www.FlowerpotPress.com
DJS-0912-0182
ISBN: 978-1-4867-1554-1
Made in China/Fabriqué en Chine

STOMP

Written by
UNCLE IAN AURORA

Illustrated by
NaTalia MOORe

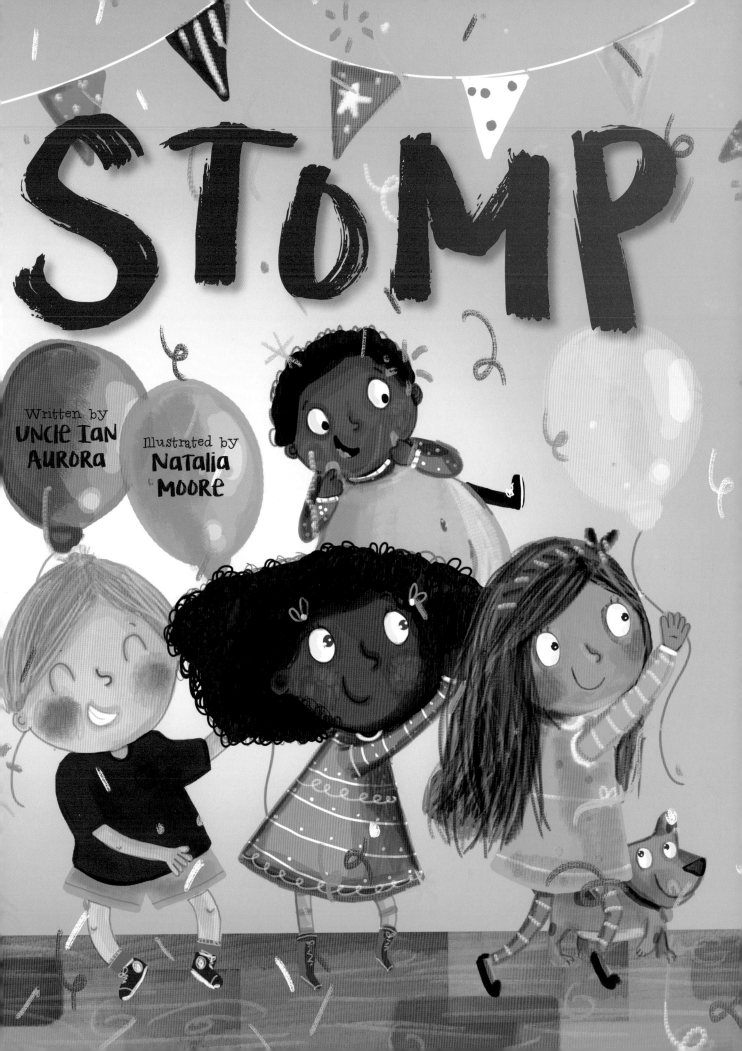

EVERYBODY UP! IT'S TIME TO GET MOVING!

NOW REPEAT AFTER ME...

STOMP 1, 2.

STOMP
1, 2, 3.

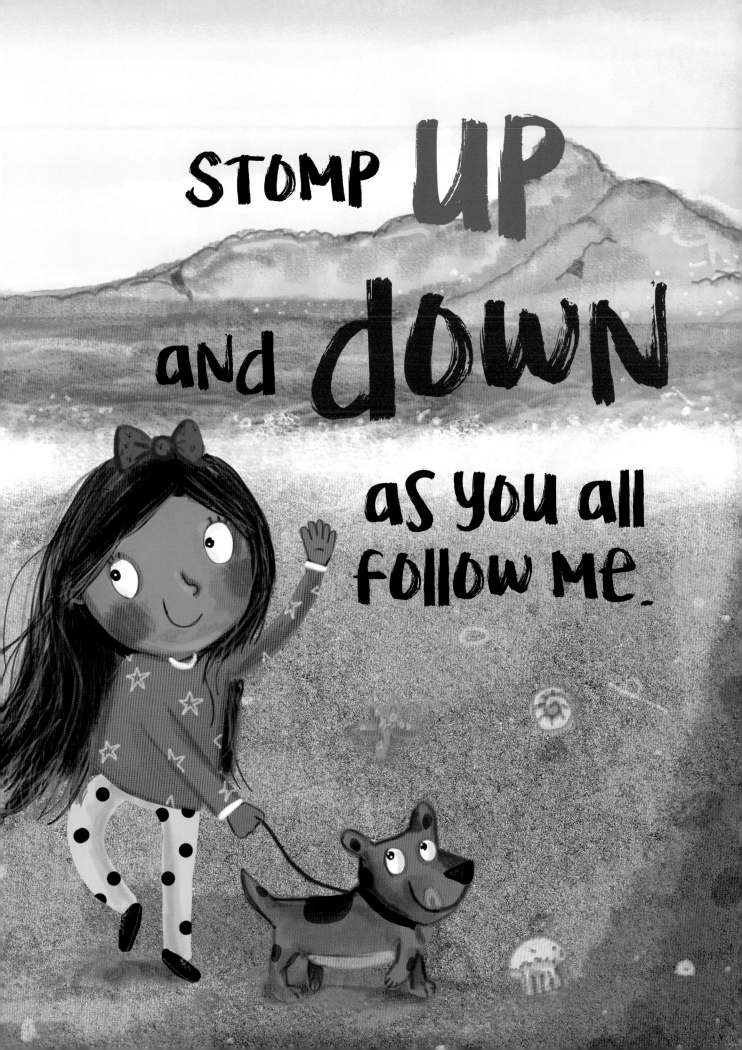

STOMP TO THE
left.

wave your
fingertips.

STOMP TO THE RIGHT.

MOVE YOUR KNEES AND YOUR HIPS.

STOMP Really
Slow
while you move
This way.

STOMP REALLY **fast**

like you need TO RUN away.

STOMP just a little

as you wiggle all YOUR TOES.

STOMP SIX TIMES

while you're tapping
on your nose.

SOMETIMES WE STOMP
WHEN IT'S TIME TO
CREATE.

by Mary

SOMETIMES WE STOMP WHEN IT'S TIME TO celebRATE

STOP FOR a
SECOND,
STRETCH YOUR
body REally wide.

Now do a
goofy
STOMP

Pat YOUR head and Make it Shake.

FINALLY, STOMP a

happy

dance

NOW THAT WE'RE all

wide awake!

THANKS FOR a GREAT STOMP!!!